My Friend Jacob

My Friend Jacob

by LUCILLE CLIFTON

illustrated by THOMAS Di GRAZIA

E. P. Dutton   New York

Library of Congress Cataloging in Publication Data

Clifton, Lucille, date   My friend Jacob.

SUMMARY: A young boy tells about Jacob, who, though
older and mentally slower, helps him a lot and is his
very best friend.
[1. Friendship—Fiction.   2. Mentally handicapped—
Fiction]   I. DiGrazia, Thomas.   II. Title.
PZ7.C6224Myk   [E]   79-19168   ISBN: 0-525-35487-5

Published in the United States by E. P. Dutton, a Division
of Elsevier-Dutton Publishing Company, Inc., New York

Published simultaneously in Canada by Clarke,
Irwin & Company Limited, Toronto and Vancouver

Editor: Ann Durell   Designer: Claire Counihan

Printed in the U.S.A.   First Edition
10 9 8 7 6 5 4 3 2 1

for my friend D.

My best friend lives next door. His name is Jacob. He is my very very best friend.

We do things together, Jacob and me. We love to play basketball together. Jacob always makes a basket on the first try.

He helps me to learn how to hold the ball so that I can make baskets too.

My mother used to say "Be careful with Jacob and that ball; he might hurt you." But now she doesn't. She knows that Jacob wouldn't hurt anybody, especially his very very best friend.

I love to sit on the steps and watch the cars go by with Jacob. He knows the name of every kind of car. Even if he only sees it just for a minute, Jacob can tell you the kind of car.

He is helping me be able to tell the cars too. When I make a mistake, Jacob never ever laughs. He just says, "No no, Sam, try again."

And I do. He is my best best friend.

When I have to go to the store, Jacob goes with me to help me. His mother used to say "You don't have to have Jacob tagging along with you like that, Sammy." But now she doesn't. She knows we like to go to the store together. Jacob helps me to carry, and I help Jacob to remember.

"Red is for stop," I say if Jacob forgets.
"Green is for go."
"Thank you, Sam," Jacob always says.

Jacob's birthday and my birthday are two days apart. Sometimes we celebrate together.

Last year he made me a surprise. He had been having a secret for weeks and weeks, and my mother knew, and his mother knew, but they wouldn't tell me.

Jacob would stay in the house in the afternoon for half an hour every day and not say anything to me when he came out. He would just smile and smile.

On my birthday, my mother made a cake for me with eight candles, and Jacob's mother made a cake for him with seventeen candles. We sat on the porch and sang and blew out our candles. Jacob blew out all of his in one breath because he's bigger.

Then my mother smiled and Jacob's
mother smiled and said, "Give it to him,
Jacob dear." My friend Jacob smiled and
handed me a card.

HAPPY BIRTHDAY SAM
JACOB

He had printed it all himself! All by
himself, my name and everything! It was
neat!

My very best friend Jacob does so much
helping me, I wanted to help him too. One day
I decided to teach him how to knock.

Jacob will just walk into somebody's house if
he knows them. If he doesn't know them, he
will stand by the door until somebody notices
him and lets him in.

"I wish Jacob would knock on the door," I heard my mother say.

So I decided to help him learn. Every day I would tell Jacob, but he would always forget. He would just open the door and walk right in.

My mother said probably it was too hard for him and I shouldn't worry about it. But I felt bad because Jacob always helped me so much, and I wanted to be able to help him too.

I kept telling him and he kept forgetting, so one day I just said, "Never mind, Jacob, maybe it is too hard."

"What's the matter, Sam?" Jacob asked me.

"Never mind, Jacob" was all I said.

Next day, at dinnertime, we were sitting in our dining room when me and my mother and my father heard this real loud knocking at the door. Then the door popped open and Jacob stuck his head in.

"I'm knocking, Sam!" he yelled.

Boy, I jumped right up from the table and went grinning and hugged Jacob, and he grinned and hugged me too. He is my very very very best friend in the whole wide world!

LUCILLE CLIFTON has written many books for children, including *Amifika, Don't You Remember?*, and *The Black B C's.* She wrote this one because she has a young friend like Jacob who, "like all people who are a bit short on one side, is quite tall on others" and who wants to be treated the same as everyone else. Mrs. Clifton, who lives in Baltimore, Maryland, has recently been named the state's poet laureate.

THOMAS DiGRAZIA is a poet as well as an illustrator. He first collaborated with Lucille Clifton on *Amifika,* and has most recently illustrated *Holiday Tales of Sholom Aleichem* in a new translation by Aliza Shevrin (Scribner's). He and his family live in New York City.

The display type is Baskerville photolettering. The text type is Primer Fototronic. The art was drawn in pencil, and the book was printed by offset at Halliday Lithograph.